Farmyard Beat

Farmyard Beat

by
Lindsey Craig

illustrations by
Marc Brown

SCHOLASTIC INC.

For my amazing family
—L.C.

For our lovely dancing Isabella
—M.B.

No part of this publication may be reproduced, stored in a retrieval system, or transmitted in any form or by any means, electronic, mechanical, photocopying, recording, or otherwise, without written permission of the publisher. For information regarding permission, write to Alfred A. Knopf, an imprint of Random House Children's Books, a division of Penguin Random House LLC, 1745 Broadway, New York, NY 10019.

ISBN 978-1-338-28892-6

Text copyright © 2011 by Lindsey Craig.
Cover art and interior illustrations copyright © 2011 by Marc Brown.
All rights reserved.
Published by Scholastic Inc., 557 Broadway, New York, NY 10012,
by arrangement with Alfred A. Knopf, an imprint of
Random House Children's Books, a division of Penguin Random House LLC.
SCHOLASTIC and associated logos are trademarks and/or
registered trademarks of Scholastic Inc.

The publisher does not have any control over and does not assume
any responsibility for author or third-party websites or their content.

12 11 10 9 8 7 6 5 4 3 2 18 19 20 21 22 23

Printed in the U.S.A. 40

First Scholastic printing, October 2018

The text of this book is set in Arthur.

The illustrations in this book were created using
hand-painted papers and a collage technique that focused on
cutting the paper into primary shapes.

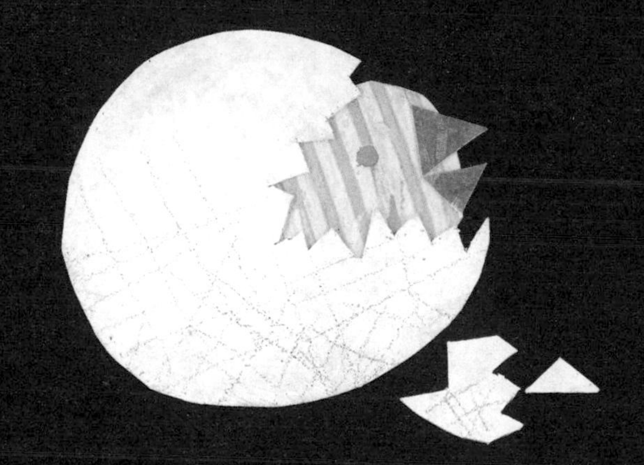

Peep-peep-peep!

Chicks can't sleep. Chicks can't sleep.
Chicks can't sleep
'cause they got that beat!

Peep! Peep! Peep-peep-peep!

Peep! Peep! Peep-peep-peep!

All that peeping wakes up . . .

Sheep!
Sheep can't sleep.
Sheep can't sleep.
Sheep can't sleep
'cause they got that beat.

TAT! TAT! Tattity-tat-tat!

TAT! TAT! Tattity-tat-tat!

All that racket wakes up . . .

Cat!
Cat can't sleep.
Cat can't sleep.
Cat can't sleep
'cause she's got that beat.

Puuurrrrr! Mee-ooow!

Puuurrrrr! Mee-ooow!

All that racket wakes up . . .

Cow!
Cows can't sleep.
Cows can't sleep.
Cows can't sleep
'cause they got that beat.

SWISH! CLANK! Swish-swish! Clank!

SWISH! CLANK! Swish-swish! Clank!

All that racket wakes Ol' . . .

Hank!
Hank can't sleep.
Hank can't sleep.
Hank can't sleep
'cause he's got that beat.

Woof! How-WOOOOO!

Woof! How-WOOOOO!

All that racket wakes up . . .

Shhh! Shhh!
Look who's coming!

WHOOO? WHOOO?
Lantern swinging . . .
WHOOO? WHOOO?

FARMER SUE!!!

Sue can't sleep.

Sue can't sleep.

Sue can't sleep

'cause she's heard that beat.

Sue looks here! Sue looks there!

"No one here or anywhere!"

With a y-a-w-n, she thinks she'll go to sleep

when . . .

Peep! Peep!
Peep-peep-peep!
Chicks can't help it.
They got that beat!
Then . . .

TAT! TAT! Tattity-tat-tat!

Puuurrrr! Mee-ooow!

SWISH! CLANK! Swish-swish! Clank!

Woof! How-WOOOOO!

WHOOO? WHOOO?

JIG! JIG! A-jiggity-jig!

Everyone's dancing to that beat.

T-I-L-L . . .

. . . they fall in a heap!

Asleep!

Cock-a-doodle-doo!
I've got that beat!

Lindsey Craig made her picture-book debut with the acclaimed *Dancing Feet!*, illustrated by Marc Brown. She has also written a musical, *Cinderella's Shakespeare*, which is performed nationwide. She lives with her husband and two children on a small island in Washington State.

Marc Brown is the creator of Arthur, the aardvark star of many picture books and a six-time Emmy Award-winning PBS television show. He is also the illustrator of many books for children, including the *New York Times* bestsellers *Wild About Books* and *Born to Read* by Judy Sierra. He lives on Martha's Vineyard and in New York City.